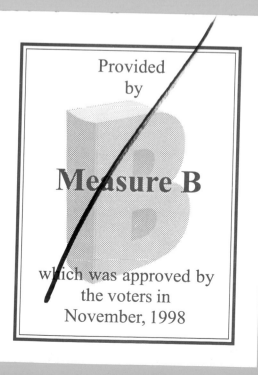

Provided
by

Measure B

which was approved by
the voters in
November, 1998

OTTO
Goes to Camp

Todd PARR

Megan Tingley Books

LITTLE, BROWN AND COMPANY

New York • An AOL Time Warner Company

To Jerry and Bully—I love you very much
—Me

Also by Todd Parr

Copyright © 2004 by Todd Parr

First Edition

Library of Congress Cataloging-in-Publication Data

Parr, Todd.
    Otto goes to camp / Todd Parr.—1st ed.
      p. cm.
    Summary: When Otto goes to camp, everyone else makes fun of the things he has brought along, but one of those things comes in very handy.
    ISBN 0-316-73900-6
    [1. Camping—Fiction. 2. Dogs—Fiction.] I. Title.
PZ7.P2447 Os 2004
[E]—dc21   2003044689

10 9 8 7 6 5 4 3 2 1

TWP

Printed in Singapore

Otto is going to camp for the first time. He is excited, but he is also worried about missing home.

"I know," says Otto.
"I'll bring all my favorite
things with me. Then
camp will be just like
home." So Otto brings...

his blanket,

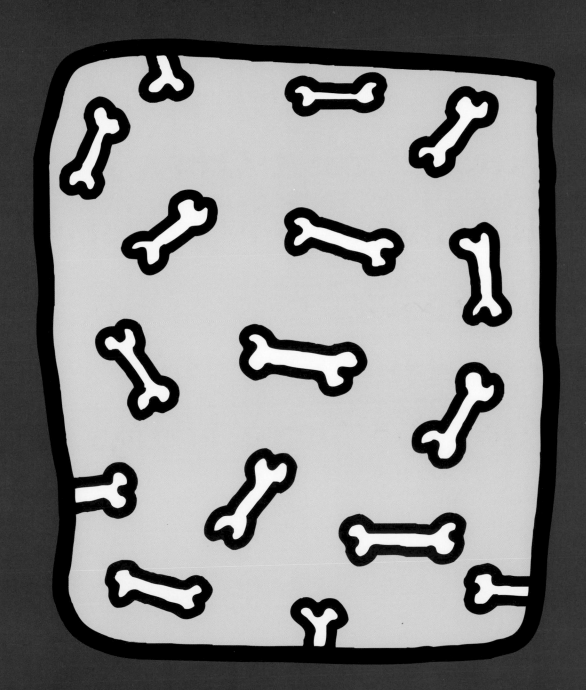

his bone,

his stick,

and a cherry pie.

Silly Otto!

Otto arrives at camp
with all of his things.

The first day, everybody goes fishing. But Otto doesn't catch anything.

"Silly Otto," say the other campers. "Fish don't like bones!"

That night, they roast marshmallows. But Otto keeps burning his. "Your stick is too short," say the other campers. "Silly Otto!"

When it's time for bed,
Otto lies on his blanket.
"You're supposed to be in
a sleeping bag," say the
other campers.

But when Otto goes into his sleeping bag, he gets stuck. "Silly Otto!"

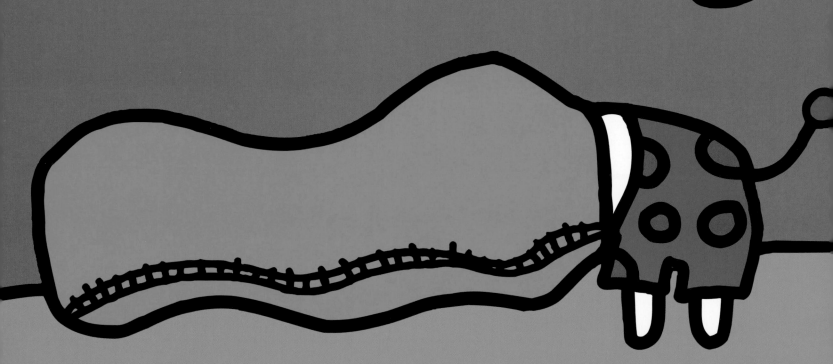

Maybe tomorrow will be better, he thinks. Finally, Otto falls asleep under the stars.

The next day the campers go on a hike. Otto packs his blanket, his bone, his stick, and his cherry pie. "Silly Otto!"

Suddenly, the campers run into a bear. "Eek!" they all yell.

But Otto isn't scared. He likes bears.

"Hello, Bear," says Otto. "How are you?"

"I'm hungry," says the bear.

Otto takes his cherry pie out of his backpack. "Would you like some?" he asks.

"Yum!" says the bear. "Cherry pie is my favorite."

"Smart Otto!" say the campers. Otto spreads out his blanket and they all have a picnic.

"I can't wait to come back next year!" says Otto.

Always bring your favorite toy 🦴 with you wherever you go so you won't feel lonely.
Love, OTTo and Todd